THIS WALKER BOOK BELONGS TO:

_____

_____

_____

_____

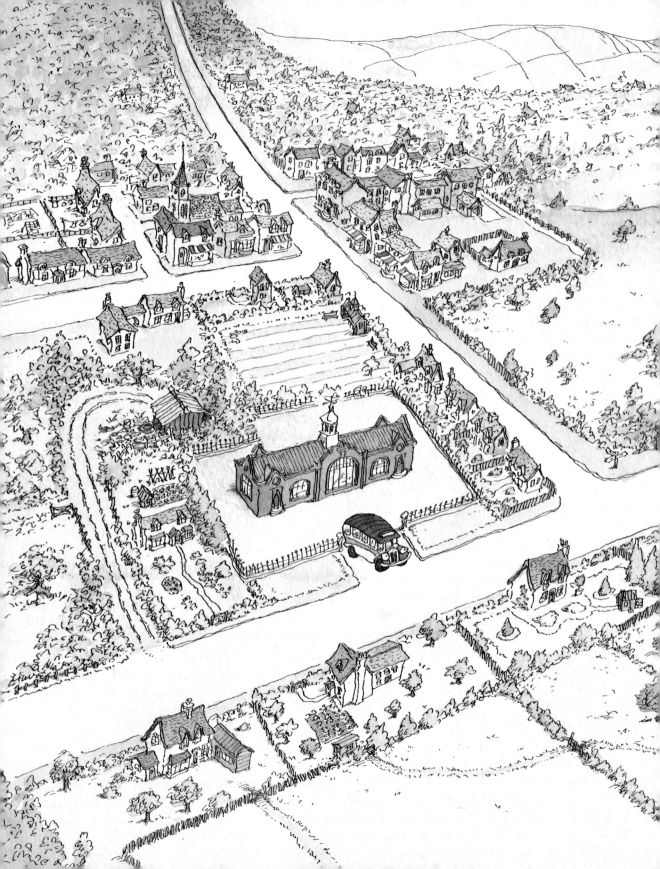

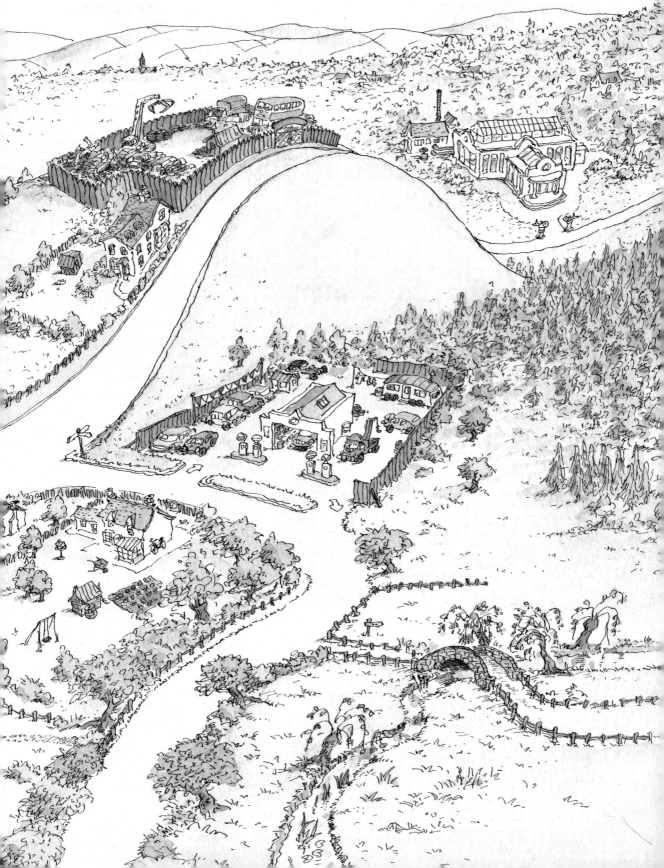

First published 1992 by
Walker Books Ltd, 87 Vauxhall Walk
London SE11 5HJ

Text © 1992 Jon Blake
Illustrations © 1992 Arthur Robins

This edition published 1994

Printed and bound by
Dai Nippon Printing Co. (HK) Ltd

This book has been typeset in Plantin.

British Library Cataloguing in Publication Data
A catalogue record for this book is
available from the British Library.
ISBN 0-7445-3144-6

IMPO

Written by
Jon Blake

Illustrated by
Arthur Robins

WALKER BOOKS
LONDON

In a dark shed, at the very back of the
school, lived a worn-out old bus.
On the front of this bus was written
IMPERIAL SCHOOL BUS
but everybody called him Impo.

Every week, Impo took the boys and
girls to the swimming baths.
On the way, there was a big hill, called
Scrapyard Hill.
Impo hated hills. They made him groan
and strain and splutter.
But he hated the scrapyard even more.

One day, the boys and girls were more excited than usual. They were going on a mystery trip.
Impo didn't know where they were going. It was a mystery to him as well.

Mr Dennis drove Impo out of town.
Suddenly, there was a hill ahead. It was
the biggest hill Impo had ever seen!

Impo began to climb.
"Come on, Impo!" laughed the boys
and girls, banging on the seats.
But the hill seemed to get steeper
and steeper.
Suddenly, something went TWANG!

Thick black smoke poured from
Impo's engine.
Mr Dennis called the breakdown men.
Impo heard them whisper a terrible
word: scrapyard.
The girls and boys heard it too.

It was dark when Impo arrived at
the scrapyard.
The breakdown men parked him on
the cold, hard gravel, between a
double-decker and a minibus.

Weeks went by.
Spiders made webs on Impo's
steering wheel.
Spots of rust appeared on his bonnet.
The boys and girls drove past, in a bus
borrowed from another school.
They didn't laugh now.

Then one day, Beryl came to the
scrapyard. "I know this bus!" she said.
"This bus took me to the baths when
I was a girl!"
The next he knew, Impo was being
towed away to a strange garage.
Beryl opened his bonnet, with a
spanner in her hand.
Impo felt his bolts being loosened,
then everything went black.

When Impo woke up, he was out in the sun.
He felt strange, but he couldn't say why.
He checked his foot-pedals, his lights and his
windscreen wipers. Everything was still there.
Then Beryl turned the key.
WROOOOOOOM!
Impo nearly jumped off his wheels.
Impo was a hot rod!

Meanwhile, the boys and girls were on their way to the baths. As they passed the scrapyard, they looked out for Impo. But Impo wasn't there.
ZOOOOOOOM! Impo was overtaking them on the other side!

When Impo finally stopped, all the boys and girls crowded round.
"Isn't he fast!" they cried.
"Too fast!" said Beryl. "He needs a heavy load to slow him down."
"What about the boys and girls?" asked Mr Dennis.
Everyone cheered.

Now Beryl drives the boys and girls to the baths every week, and Impo has a new home – at the very *front* of the school.

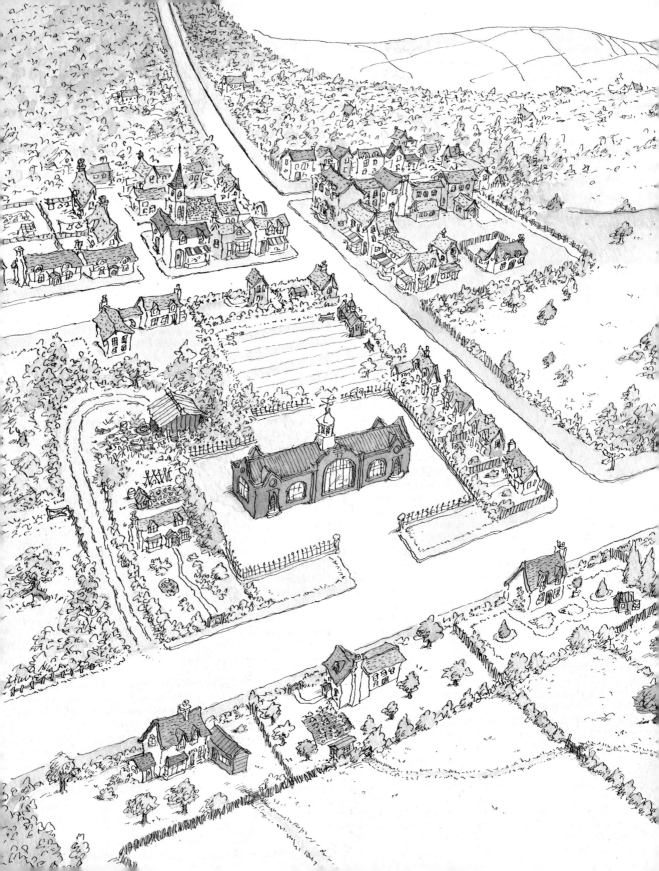

MORE WALKER PAPERBACKS
For You to Enjoy

LITTLE RABBIT FOO FOO
by Michael Rosen / Arthur Robins

A new version of a popular playground rhyme.

"Simple and hilarious... I laugh every time I think about it." *Susan Hill, The Sunday Times*

0-7445-2065-7   £3.99

THE DUMP TRUCK
THE TUGBOAT
by Arlene Blanchard and Tony Wells

Each of these intriguing books follows a hard-working machine through a busy, action-packed day.

The Dump Truck   0-7445-3119-5
The Tugboat   0-7445-3118-7
£3.99 each

TRANSPORT MACHINES
by Derek Radford

Loggers and low loaders, tankers and trailers, dustcarts and dump trucks – this colourful book is packed with different kinds of transport machines.

"Colourful, lively illustrations... The text is simple but sufficient ... delightfully entertaining." *Books for Keeps*

0-7445-2095-9   £3.99

Walker Paperbacks are available from most booksellers, or by post from Walker Books Ltd, PO Box 11, Falmouth, Cornwall TR10 9EN.

To order, send: Title, author, ISBN number and price for each book ordered, your full name and address, cheque or postal order for the total amount, plus postage and packing: UK and BFPO Customers – £1.00 for first book, plus 50p for the second book and plus 30p for each additional book to a maximum charge of £3.00. Overseas and Eire Customers – £2.00 for first book, plus £1.00 for the second book and plus 50p per copy for each additional book.
Prices are correct at time of going to press, but are subject to change without notice.